Buster Takes a Hostage

Join Buster and his gruesome crew for more piratical adventures!

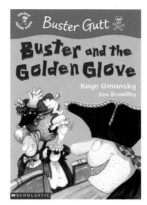

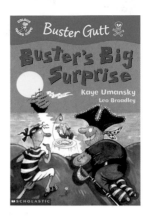

And why not try some other Colour Young Hippo titles too!

Beetle and Friends

Mermaid Rock

Millie and Bombassa

Sherlock Hound

Creepy Crawlies

Fat Alphie and Charlie the Wimp

Tales from Whispery Wood

Buster Gutt

Buster Takes a Hostage

Kaye Umansky
illustrated by Leo Broadley

This edition produced for the Book People Ltd,
Hall Wood Avenue, Haydock, St Helens WA11 9UL

First published by Scholastic Ltd, 2004

ISBN 0 439 95440 1

Printed and bound by Tien Wah Press Pte. Ltd, Singapore

"Broke," said Buster Gutt, the pirate chief, staring down into his empty treasure chest. "Not a penny, Tiddlefish. Not a bean. Where'd it all go?"

"We shouldn't have gone to Pirate Island," said Timothy Tiddlefish, the cabin boy, who always had a cold. "I said we couldn't a – *achoo!* Afford it."

Pirate Island was a popular
holiday resort in the South Seas.
It had everything a fun-loving
pirate needed – sun, sea,
hook and eye-patch stalls,
barbecued grub, unlimited rum
and a huge punch-up every evening.
Buster and the crew had spent two
glorious weeks there.

"It were a good 'oliday,
though," sighed Buster,
fingering his black eye.
"Won the punch-up cup,
didn't we?"

They both eyed the big gold cup
which had pride of place in Buster's cabin.

It had been presented to them for winning
the punch-up fourteen nights in a row.
Buster was thrilled with it and swore he
would keep it for ever.

"I suppose we'd better tell the crew," sighed Timothy. "But they're gonna be mad a – a – *achoo!*"

"Why me?" protested Buster. "We all spent it."

"Yes, but the captain's meant to look after the money. You never explained it was *all* gone."

The crew took the news very badly indeed.

"Broke?" cried
Jimmy Maggot,
the cook.

"No goin'
ashore to spend,
spend, spend?" wailed
Crasher Jackson,
the helmsman.

"No tavern
meals?" gasped
Threefingers
Jake, the bosun.

"No toppin' up on the rum?" gulped One-Eyed Ed, the lookout.

"Nope," sighed Buster. "Not till we done some lootin' an' pillagin'."

"An' what am I supposed to cook in the meantime?" demanded Jimmy Maggot. "We're out of everythin' 'cept boiled seaweed."

Everyone made a face. Boiled seaweed tasted awful, like salty knitting.

"All right, so we'll live on Bowzer's octopus scratchin's," said Buster.

Bowzer, the ship's dog, looked worried. He *loved* his octopus scratchings.

"'Tis all very well talkin' about lootin' an' pillagin', Captain," said One-Eyed Ed, "but we ain't seen any ships, 'ave we? Not for days."

This was true. Ever since leaving Pirate Island, the seas had been empty of all but the odd rock.

"Somethin'll turn up," said Buster, trying to sound confident. "Let's take a shifty through the telescope. All 'ands on deck!"

Chapter Two

Admiral Ainsley Goldglove, the celebrated
pirate-catcher, leaned back and sighed
contentedly. It had been an excellent
supper. Chicken, cherries, cheese and
champagne.

The admiral had recently rounded up a record number of pirates, getting a large purse of gold and his picture in the paper for his efforts. Right now his ship, the *HMS Glorious*, was at anchor, and he was enjoying a well-earned rest, away from the cheering crowds.

ADMIRAL GOLDGLOVE DOES IT AGAIN!

"All finished, sir? Shall I fetch your cash box?" asked Crisply Pimpleby, the first officer, saluting smartly.

The admiral nodded.

"Good idea, Pimpleby." There was nothing he liked better than sitting on deck on a summer evening, counting his money.

"I'll get Plankton to clear away the dishes," said Monty Marshmallow, the chef, and went off to find Private Derek Plankton, who was dusting somewhere.

"Excuse me, Admiral," said Seaman
Scuttle, excitedly approaching the table.
"Ship sighted on the starboard side. Could
be pirates. Shall I wheel
out the cannons?"

"Not now, Scuttle," said the admiral,
testily. "I'm not in the mood for fighting.
All that smoke and noise. I'm letting my
supper go down."

"Excellent decision, sir,"
said Crisply Pimpleby,
staggering up with
a huge chest. "It's
not as if you're
short of cash,
is it?"

He threw open the lid with a flourish.
It was filled to
the brim with
gold coins!

"*Sharksbum!* See that?" gasped Buster as they leaned over the rail, gazing at the distant ship. "It's 'im! Goldglove! Sittin' there smirkin' with a load o' posh nosh an' a *chest full o' dosh*!"

"Let's see," said Timothy Tiddlefish. He took the telescope and put it to his eye.

Sure enough, there was the *HMS Glorious*. And there was the admiral at his table, stacking gold coins into tall towers.

"It's not fair!" snarled Buster. "'Ow come 'e's got gold an' I ain't? Well, I wants some, *right now*! We'll sail up an' swarm aboard an' grab the loot an—"

"Bad idea," said Timothy.

"Eh? Why?"

"Because they'll see us coming and there'll be a big fight and we'll lose. You don't want the admiral to ca – a – *achoo!* Catch you. Do you?"

"Well, no…" growled Buster.

"Right," said Timothy. "I've got a better idea. Listen…"

Chapter Three

A big moon hung in the sky. On board the
HMS Glorious, everyone had gone to bed,
apart from Private Derek Plankton, who
was still clearing up. He had washed the
dishes and swept up the crumbs. He was
now hard at work polishing the table.

He was so busy, he didn't hear the creak of approaching oars. He only became aware that something was afoot when a blanket came down over his head and he found himself being manhandled over the side and down into a rowing boat.

When the blanket was finally removed, he found himself standing on the deck of *The Bad Joke*, surrounded by Buster's motley crew.

"Hello, Derek," said Timothy Tiddlefish. "We've taken you hostage. Sorry."

"Oh," said Private Derek Plankton. He nibbled his duster. "Will it hurt?"

"Course not," said Buster, a bit put out. "What d'you take us for?"

"Um – pirates?" guessed Private Derek Plankton. He reached down and gave Bowzer a little pat. Bowzer licked his hand.

"Well, yeah," agreed Buster. "Yeah, we're *pirates*. But we ain't got nothin' against you. 'Tis Goldglove we don't like. We're 'oldin' you ransom till 'e coughs up a hundred gold coins."

26

"We'll send you ba – a – *achoo!* – back safe and sound, as soon as it a – *achoo!* – arrives," promised Timothy.

"All right," said Private Derek Plankton, with a shrug. "What'll I do till then?"

"Whatever you like, long as you don't try to escape," said Buster. "Bowzer! Guard the prisoner."

Bowzer wagged his tail. He loved Private Derek Plankton.

It wasn't until the following morning that Admiral Ainsley Goldglove discovered Private Derek Plankton gone and a ransom note pinned to the mast with a dagger.
It read:

"See this?" raged the admiral. "What a cheek!"

"Dear me," said Crisply Pimpleby. "This is a bad business. Will you pay up, sir?"

"What, and let Gutt get one over on me? Certainly not! Man the cannons! We'll sink his ship."

"But what about Plankton? He'll sink with it," said Crisply Pimpleby, uneasily.

"So?"

"But it's not done, sir, sinking one of your own men. What if the papers find out?"

"Hmm." The admiral looked thoughtful. "All right, forget the cannon. But I'm not paying a penny. I shall play a waiting game. And in the meantime, *you* can do the cleaning."

Chapter Four

Back on board *The Bad Joke*, Buster had just
got a bad surprise. "Oh no!" he groaned.
"Look what 'e's done to my ship!"

The Bad Joke was unrecognizable. It
gleamed. It shone. It had been dusted,
swept, scrubbed and buffed. The holes in
the sails had been neatly mended. Even
Bowzer had been given a bath!

Right now, Private Derek Plankton was high up the rigging, rehanging the Jolly Roger which had been washed, ironed and dyed pink.

"He must have been a – *achoo!* – at it all night," gasped Timothy.

"You should see my galley!" wailed Jimmy Maggot. "He's scraped the burnt bits off the pots! I liked them burnt bits. The burnt bits is where you get all the flavour."

"He put a vase o' flowers in my cabin," growled Crasher Jackson. "*Flowers!* Where'd he get flowers in the middle of the ocean?"

"I keep falling over, where he's oiled the deck," complained One-Eyed Ed, rubbing his shin. "He's dangerous, he is."

"Any news about the ransom?" Buster asked Timothy Tiddlefish, hopefully.

"No," said Timothy, glumly.

"Perhaps we're askin' too much," said Buster. "Perhaps we should take a bit less."

Everyone agreed that perhaps a hundred gold coins *was* a bit much.

Some time later, on board the *HMS Glorious,*
Crisply Pimpleby trailed up and presented
the admiral with a soggy piece of paper.

"What's this?" snapped the admiral.

"Another message from Gutt, sir.
Arrived in a bottle."

Crisply Pimpleby stifled a yawn. Cleaning was *hard*. His back hurt. He had accidentally squirted polish in his eye. The frilly apron didn't suit him.

However hard he tried, he simply couldn't keep up with the mess. He hoped Private Derek Plankton would be released soon.

The admiral snatched the note. It read:

AWL RITE

50

Over on *The Bad Joke*, Private Derek
Plankton was polishing cannonballs and
arranging them in a tidy pile.

"I'm gonna stop 'im," announced Buster.
"I can't stand watchin', it's drivin' me mad."

"You said he could – *achoo!* – do whatever he liked," Timothy reminded him.

"Well, I've changed me mind. Either 'e stops cleanin' or 'e goes overboard."

"Then we won't have a hostage," Timothy pointed out.

"So? Ain't no sign o' the ransom."

"Perhaps fifty's pushin' it a bit," said Threefingers Jake. "Maybe we should go for thirty?"

"Try for twenty," moaned Crasher Jackson. "Let's get rid of 'im."

"Ten," pleaded One-Eyed Ed. "Just to be on the safe side."

"Ten it is, then," sighed Buster, and he stomped off to his cabin to write yet another ransom note.

☠ ☠ ☠

"Another one's arrived sir," yawned Crisply Pimpleby. "Dropped by a seagull this time." Tiredly, he held out the note, which read:

"You see?" chortled the admiral. "He's cracking!"

"Can't we pay up, sir?" pleaded Crisply Pimpleby. He had just finished scrubbing the deck, only to find a flock of seagulls had undone all his good work.

"No chance," said the admiral. "We stick to our guns. Or in your case, the mop. Come along, man, get cleaning! That deck's a disgrace!"

A short time later, another note arrived, by arrow this time.

"Down to five, I see," said the admiral, crumpling it up and throwing it into the sea.

He did the same to the next four.

That night, when darkness fell, a small rowing boat nudged against the stern of the *HMS Glorious*. In it, was Private Derek Plankton. Pinned on his hat was a final message. It read:

The next morning everyone was pleased to find Private Derek Plankton back on board ship.

"Well done, Plankton," said the admiral. "You kept your head and saved me money. I feel a small reward is in order. What would you like?"

Private Derek Plankton thought about it. "Well, I could do with a new duster."

Back on board *The Bad Joke*, Buster and the boys sat gloomily on deck, eating boiled seaweed. The ship was spick and span and smelled of lemons.

"I 'ates it," grumbled Buster. "Don't feel like 'ome any more."

"Cheer up, Captain," said Timothy, consolingly. "We'll soon mess it up again."

"All that, and we're still broke," said Buster.

"Ah well. You win some, you – *achoo!* – lose some. What do we do now?"

Buster gave a little sigh. His eyes flickered around the cabin and landed on his favourite thing. "The way I see it," he said, "there's only one thing we *can* do."

So this is what they did. They sailed back to Pirate Island ...

... sold the punch-up cup to a rival crew ...

... spent the proceeds on another rip-roaring holiday ...

… and ended up
broke again!

The
Dragon
Test

Written by June Crebbin

Illustrated by Polly Dunbar

WALKER BOOKS
AND SUBSIDIARIES

LONDON · BOSTON · SYDNEY

2nd May

Dear Poppa King,
    I don't like it here. The castle
is so big. I keep getting lost. I wish
I was back with you at the palace.
    Lots and lots of love,
    Jem xxxxxxxx

castle

me

3

6th May

Dear Poppa King,

I know I said I wanted to take the dragon test. But it's not easy. Today we started dragon skills—that means practising things we'll need to pass the dragon test.

Sir John took us to the Great Hall and gave us a map. We had to find the kitchens. I ended up in the dungeons! They were SPOOKY—dark and cold and full of spiders.

Your very, very loving daughter,
Jem xxxxxxxxx x x x x x

PS I still miss you.

8th May

Dear Poppa King,
   Are you sure Princesses
always wear dresses? When we
practised sword-fighting today —
another dragon skill we might
need — My dress kept blowing

12th May ✿

Dear Poppa King,

   THANK YOU for the trousers.
They're a bit big but much better
than a dress.

      Today we had "Using a Lance".

whoosh! →

A target is tied to a post. You have to
run — much easier in trousers — and hit it
with your lance exactly in the middle.

If you don't, it spins round and a bag
of flour tied to the back hits you on
the head!

19th May

Dear Poppa king,
    There are so many things to learn
to be a Dragon Catcher! Today we had
rope practice. You have to throw a piece
of rope, which has a loop at one end,
over a dragon's head. (Of course the
dragon's head is a wooden one tied
to the top of a post.)

23rd May

Dragon skills learnt so far:

✦ 1. Using a map – to find a dragon.

✦ 2. Using a sword – to show the dragon who's in charge.

✦ 3. Using a lance – to prod and poke the dragon if needed.

✦ 4. Using a rope – to catch a dragon.

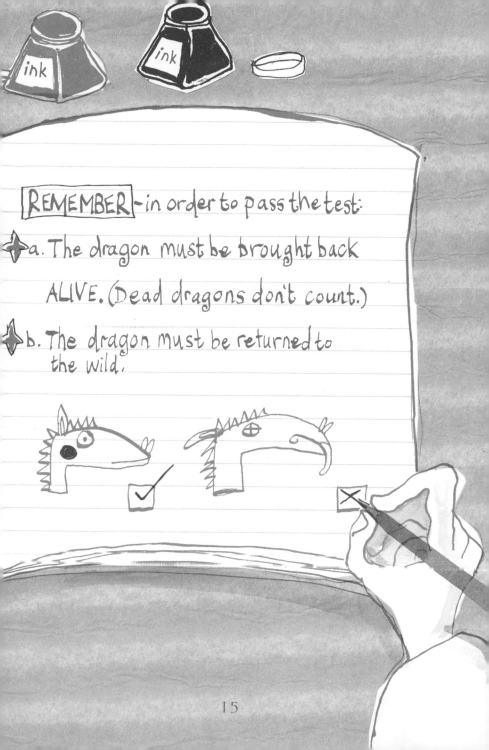

REMEMBER -in order to pass the test:

✦a. The dragon must be brought back

ALIVE. (Dead dragons don't count.)

✦b. The dragon must be returned to
the wild.

🌼 24th May 🌼

Dear Poppa king,
Did you know there are FIFTEEN different kinds of dragon ?!! We are learning about the Scaly Dragon, the sort we have to capture. We have to know where to find it, how to recognize it and how it attacks.

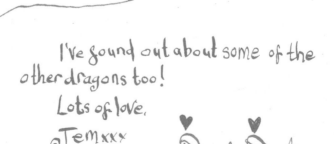

I've found out about some of the other dragons too!
Lots of love,
Jem xxx
🌼 🌼

Dragons of the World

Scaly Dragon

Description: Related to mountain dragon, though smaller and unable to fly. Green scales cover body. Red spikes on head and along backbone.
Habitat: Hills and moorland. Cave-dweller.
Habits: Breathes fire up to ten paces. Hisses and whistles when angry.
Danger rating: ∗ ∗

SEA DRAGON

Description: Striped body, flat webbed feet.
Habitat: Seashore, sand dunes.
Habits: Swims well. Enjoys eating crabs, lobster and mermaids.
Danger rating: *

MOUNTAIN DRAGON

Description: Largest known dragon. Green body, red spikes on head and along backbone. Very sharp teeth. Strong claws. Strong wings.
Habitat: Mountains. Cave-dweller.
Habits: Breathes fire up to fifty paces. Roars if woken from sleep. Attacks at once.
Danger rating: * * * * *

GREATER-SPOTTED DRAGON

Description: Pale pink body with enormous spots.
Habitat: Moist dark woods.
Habits: Climbs and leaps well. Glides rather than flies. Uses long strong tail to whip attackers.
Danger rating: * * *

THREE-HORNED MARSH DRAGON

Description: Red/brown body. Three horns on head. Short stumpy tail.
Habitat: Swamps, marshes.
Habits: Submerges itself in marshes to sleep. Grunts and squeals when attacked.
Danger rating: * *

26th May

Dear Poppa King,
    Guess what? At last we have
been riding! I thought it was never
going to happen. My horse, Fly, is fast
but she is scared of rabbits. Goodness
knows what she'll be like when she sees
a dragon!
    Heaps of love,
    Jem

30th May

Dear Poppa King,

    Sir John says I have to stick with Fly. She still jumps every time a rabbit pops up.

    But I've had an idea. This afternoon, when it's riding practice, I'm going to take Fly into the hills to find a dragon. She has to... meet one before the test. How... can I catch a dragon if she won't go near one?

    Don't worry, I know what I'm doing.

Love,
Jem   x x x

To the King,

    Your daughter, Princess Jemima, is safe. But I am very, very hungry. If you want to see your daughter alive again, bring one thousand gold coins to my cave. Come alone or I will eat her.

    From A. Scaly-Dragon

PS I've marked my cave on the map.

TO: GENERAL BATTLE

Assemble the Royal Guard.
Princess Jemima is being
held by a dangerous
dragon.
We ride at dawn.

By order: King William

31st May. Midnight. 🌙✦✦🌙✦
The Cave

♔

Dear Poppa king,   🥚🥚🥚

        I've been captured by a dragon!
It all happened so suddenly. One minute
Fly and I were cantering along, and the
next a dragon jumped out on us from
behind a rock. Poor Fly was so frightened.
She reared up and I fell off. Then the
dragon shot flames at me and forced
me into its cave.

I know you'll want to send the Royal Guard to rescue me, but PLEASE DON'T. I still want to pass the dragon test. I'll think of something.

Lots of love,
Jem ×××××

Ps You can trust the Firebird. She's the dragon's servant but she's my friend.

TO: GENERAL BATTLE

Cancel the Royal Guard.
But put up this poster.

By order: King William

1st June

The Castle

Your Majesty,

I beg to inform you
that your daughter, Princess
Jemima, has disappeared
with my horse, Fly. I must
ask you to buy another horse
at once to replace Fly, who
was a very valuable animal.

Sir John Brassneque

Sir John Brassneque DC

2nd June
The Cave

Dear Poppa King,
    Thank you for cancelling the Royal Guard. But PLEASE take down the poster, too. I don't want to be rescued by ANYONE.
    I told the dragon a STORY! He loved it. He wanted another and another. So I told him all the stories you used to tell me. I've told him forty-four stories so far. If I can just keep going until tomorrow—the day of the dragon test—I think I can persuade him to come back to the castle with me. There's more than one way to catch a dragon!
    Your loving daughter,
    Jem

STORIES TO TELL THE DRAGON
(continued)

- 45. Red Riding Hood

- 46. The Princess and the Pea

- 47. St George and the Dragon

- 47. Jack and the Beanstalk

- 48. Cinderella

- 49. The Elves and the Shoemaker

- 50. "Once upon a time there was a scaly Dragon called Arthur..."

☼ 4th June ☼ ✦

Dear Poppa King,
    I'm back at the castle! I promised
Arthur a special story if he'd come back
to the castle with me. And he agreed!
I didn't have to put a rope on him or
anything.

♡

Fly was waiting outside the cave so we all travelled back together. Sir John was surprised to see us!

Heaps of love,
x ❤ x Jem ❤ x ❤ x ❤ x

Ps The special story is called "Arthur scaly-Dragon Saves the Day."

41

THE DRAGON TEST

This is to certify that

Princess Jemima
· ·

has captured a dragon,
brought it back to the castle
and returned it to the wild.
Signed:

Sir John Brassneque
Sir John Brassneque DC

1st July

Dear Arthur,

I miss you, too. Of course you can come and stay. All that silly nonsense about eating me is quite forgotten.

I've started the new story I promised you. It's called "Arthur Scaly-Dragon to the Rescue!"

Lots of love,
Your friend,
Jem xxxx

For Anna
J.C.
For Lowdy Brabyn
P.D.

Walker Starters

The Dragon Test by June Crebbin, illustrated by Polly Dunbar
0-7445-90183
Hal the Highwayman by June Crebbin, illustrated by Polly Dunbar
0-7445-9019-1
Cup Run by Martin Waddell, illustrated by Russell Ayto
0-7445-9026-4
Going Up! by Martin Waddell, illustrated by Russell Ayto
0-7445-9027-2
Big Wig by Colin West
0-7445-90175
Percy the Pink by Colin West
0-7445-9054-X

Series consultant: Jill Bennett, author of
Learning to Read with Picture Books

First published 2003 by
Walker Books Ltd
87 Vauxhall Walk
London SE11 5HJ

10 9 8 7 6 5 4 3 2

Text © 2003 June Crebbin
Illustrations © 2003 Polly Dunbar

This book has been typeset in
Alpha Normal, Calligraph 810 BT,
Helvetica, M Garamond and
Sanvito Multiple Master

Handlettering by Polly Dunbar

Printed in Hong Kong

British Library Cataloguing in Publication Data:
a catalogue record for this book is available
from the British Library

ISBN 0-7445-90183